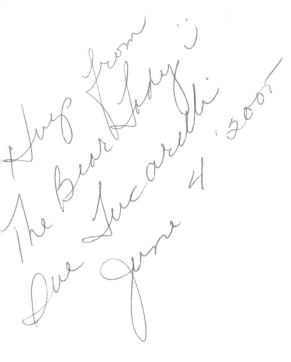

Hug from
The Bear Lady :)
Sue Tucarelli
June 4, 2005

ISBN 0-932529-80-1

OldCastle Publishing
P.O. Box 1193
Escondido, CA 92033
760-489-0336
FAX 760-747-1198

Text © Sue Lucarelli 2004
Illustrations © A. B. Curtiss 2004
Printed in China
Lucarelli, Sue.
    T. Bear's tale : Hugs Across America / by Sue
Lucarelli ; edited by A.B. Curtiss ; illustrated by
Mirto Golino. -- 1st ed.
    p. cm.
    SUMMARY: A feisty bear wants to be chosen by the Bear
Lady who has handed out 58,000 teddy bears to New York
City school children after 9-11.
    Audience: Ages 4-8.
    ISBN 0-932529-80-1

    1. Teddy bears--Juvenile fiction .2.September 11
Terrorist Attacks, 2001--Juvenile fiction. 3.Hugs
Across America (Organization)--Juvenile fiction.
(1. Teddy bears--Fiction. 2.September 11 Terrorist
Attacks'2001--Fiction.3.Hugs Across America
(Organization)--Fiction. I. Curtiss, A. B. II.
Golino, Mirto. III. Title.

PZ7.L96847Tbe 2004

Dedication

This book is dedicated to the children; the children of my class whose hugs have comforted thousands, the children of The Churchill School whose spirit gave birth to this story, the children of New York City whose lives were touched by tragedy and the children of our world who need the hope found in the arms of a teddy bear.

Acknowledgements

In the writing of this Tale, I have been helped by many whose hearts, minds, skills and endless patience have been sorely needed.

To the fellow volunteers and committed friends of Hugs Across America, without whom teddy bears would not have found their way to the hearts of children in need, I am forever grateful. To the members of the Manhasset Community Reformed Church, whose spirit and love have been the hands and feet in this phenomenal miracle of 58,000 teddy bears and my own sustenance; to Jeff Barker whose friendship, encouragement and wisdom were sources of hope from the books inception, and whose play "September Bears" gave voice and soul to our story; to his son, Daniel Barker, for his creative efforts on our behalf; to my dear friends, Mary Clark, Lucy Duer, Fran Perlstein, Regina Papa, Linda Price, Janet Stevens, and Marion Hashmet who listened intently and offered insight and patient concern;

To Meryl Schwartz, my original and tolerant editor, and to Arline Curtiss, editor and publisher, whose suggestions and thoughtfulness gave greater meaning to the written word as she so willingly supported the telling of this Tale; to my mentor, Dr. Angelo Dispenzieri, whose guidance brought me light and most especially; to my family, Nick, Elizabeth and Johnny, for their loving support and understanding, without which this story might never have occurred let alone been told, and lastly; to the children of The Churchill School who so eagerly gave their love to other children in the belief that they too could make a difference; and to the children of my class on September 11, 2001, Eden Bellow, Talia Bromberg, Erin Dacey, David Greenblatt, Sam Herscher, Daniel Nissani, Jodi Rapchik, Sophie Ratner, Daniel Shaffer, Francesca Wagner, Des Yazejian, and Alexandra Varacchi whose courage and faith were a constant inspiration, I extend my deepest gratitude.

T.Bear's Tale

Hugs Across America

Written by Sue Lucarelli
Illustrated by Mirto Golino

Edited by A. B. Curtiss

Hello! I'm so glad you're reading this book. Now I can tell you the story about T. Bear. It's a true story, you know, not just a bear story.

It's about one terrible day in September that everybody now calls 9-11, and it's about some powerful goodness that happened later. Teddy bears can't really talk, of course. Or can they? What do you think?

Now T. Bear was a very special bear. You know that's his name because it's on a tag right around his neck. He was named by a little boy who sent him to New York City with a note in his pocket that said:

I am sorry for what happened,
But T. Bear is here to snuggle
and care,
And let you know he has love
to share.
        Love,
        Jeff

T. Bear, and Gruff and Cuddles and all the other teddy bears are getting ready for the most exciting adventure of their lives. They are going to meet the Bear Lady.

But there's a big problem. T. Bear doesn't think that Gruff is ready to go, and of course Gruff is disappointed!

"T. Bear, I want to help too. Look at me! I'm a big, scary bear! Grrrrr! You can see my teeth, and my big paws with my long claws. Send me to New York City, or wherever I'm needed. I'll fight to protect the children. Grrrrr!"

"Sorry Gruff, but helping children feel better isn't about fighting, or being strong or fierce. It's about being kind.

Cuddles has a chance. She's very gentle and never scares the children. She loves to be hugged and she listens to everything they tell her, don't you, Cuddles?"

"That's very nice of you to say so, T. Bear."

"Well, it's true! You will help some child feel really safe whenever they are scared."

"Aw, T. Bear, come on!" said Gruff, "I'll bet the Bear Lady wants us to be powerful and strong. And who is she anyway? How come she gets to decide which of us bears gets to go to the schools?"

"You don't know about the Bear Lady, Gruff? She's a teacher in New York City. All her students were there, you know, on 9-11, when the Twin Towers fell.

They saw the Towers on their way to school. Then in a flash everything turned dark from the clouds of smoke. And when the smoke cleared, the Twin Towers were gone.

Those two big beautiful buildings that once stretched up to the sky were just white ash. Some children saw it happen, Cuddles...yeah, saw the planes!

The children just could not believe it, Gruff," T. Bear whispered. They kept asking WHY? Why did this happen?

The Bear Lady tried her best to calm their fears. Daniel, one of her students, came up to her and said, 'All I know is, I need a hug!'

She gave him a hug right away and then she handed him a teddy bear so that he could have a big hug whenever he wanted one.

That is the exact moment when the whole story began.

When Daniel felt better, the teacher helped the children "rebuild" the Twin Towers out of craft sticks and paper. All their structures were soooooo great! Sophie made a great big shield around hers to keep everything bad away.

David put rubber bands around his towers so anything dangerous would just bounce right off. I think the children were trying to feel safe, don't you?" said T. Bear

"Yes," replied Gruff. "I want to help them feel safe too. Maybe I could be a really big policeman bear. Or I could be a really brave fireman bear or; well, I don't know for sure. But the children need all of us bears to help. There's just got to be a place for me too. Grrrrr!"

"But Gruff, look at you! You're always growling. The children don't need us to be tough guys. They're already upset when bad things happen like war or floods or fires. You might even scare them more. Look at those teeth, especially those teeth!"

"But listen, T. Bear. I can

fight the danger, whatever it is. I'll give it my left claw and my right claw, and see, I can...I can beat it. Grrrrr!"

"But fighting is not our job!" insisted T. Bear.

"Oh, come on, T. Bear. At least let me meet this Bear Lady. I know I can convince her. I just want to help protect the kids. Grrrrr!"

"Cuddles, what do you think?" said T. Bear. "Perhaps there is some child who really would feel safer with Gruff around. Maybe we s*hould* let the Bear Lady decide?"

"You're probably right, T. Bear. I have an idea. Let's see if we can help Gruff hide his claws. But, my goodness, what can we do with his growl, and those teeth!"

"I won't growl or show my teeth, Cuddles! I'll...I'll just keep my mouth closed. Yeah, that's it. I'll be the strong, silent type. Then the children will be calmed by my quiet strength. How's that, T. Bear, can I go?"

"Okay. Okay, Gruff. You can come with us I guess. But no trouble now, because this is a really big responsibility."

And T. Bear was so right. Listen to this letter from a soldier's child and you can see how his teddy bear is helping.

Ben's Dad is in the Army and was sent to New York City right after 9-11. Did you know there were U. S. tanks rolling down Broadway then instead of yellow taxi cabs?"

Dear Bear Lady,

I named my bear Angel, because it is the best bear ever. I miss my Dad so much. When I cry at night, I hug my bear and I remember what my Dad would want me to do. My bear is very fluffy.

Yours truly,
Ben

"See," said T. Bear. "We have to listen to our children's worries, because that's the most important thing. We have to hold them when they feel like crying. And when we hear their little hearts beat faster, we have to squeeze very tight.

"Come on everybody, let's go!" said T. Bear as he raced ahead Our job is waiting for us."

"Where are we going?" insisted Gruff, as he ran after T. Bear. "When will we meet the Bear Lady? Will she tell me right away if I'm accepted? Come on, T. Bear, tell me, tell me please!"

"Okay. First, we'll all be packed together in a big box, taken to the Post Office and mailed to the Bear Lady's church. The people there will get us ready to meet a child who needs us.

One of them will write a special message on a card that we get to wear around our necks. You know, stuff that tells the children how much they are loved."

"WOW, T. Bear, I can hardly wait. I'm sure I'll make it. I just have to, Grrrrr. I will, won't I?"

Then T. Bear and all his friends were packed into a large box and put into a truck. When the truck started moving, who do you think was the first bear to cause trouble?

"T. Bear, I don't like this box thing, I'm all squashed, I can't even find my right paw and...and...

"Hush, Gruff. Remember? You promised that you would be the strong, *silent* type."

"Oh, T. Bear, it *is* really uncomfortable in here," sighed Cuddles. "My left ear is twisted down so hard. Hope I'll be able to hear the children's stories."

"Cuddles, I'll try to move a little so your ear can smooth out and be ready for listening."

"You are very thoughtful, T. Bear... Thanks. You know, I've been wondering. Why do you think children need us teddy bears? Why *us*, instead of some toy?"

"I know why, Cuddles. Remember Daniel? He wasn't the only child who needed a hug on 9-11. When the Bear Lady gave him a teddy bear, all the other boys and girls said they really wanted a hug too. But there were only three bears in the classroom

The Bear Lady promised that if the children would share the three teddy bears that day, the next morning she would bring a bear for each one of them. The children did share. They just kept passing those three bears back and forth to one another.

Then the Bear Lady went to her little church, it really is a very little church, and asked all her friends to bring teddy bears for the children. And they did.

The very next day the Bear Lady gave a bear to each one of her students And then another class asked for bears.

Pretty soon the whole school wanted bears to hug. The word got out and another school called, and then another and another. Children always seem to know the real truth about teddy bears, don't they?

When the Twin Towers fell everyone was so sad. But then all of us teddy bears rose up like balloons of the heart.

In those few weeks after 9-11, the Bear Lady and her friends from that very small church handed out more than 58,000 teddy bears to the children in New York City. WOW! That is a lot of hugs isn't it, Cuddles?"

Suddenly the bear friends felt their box being lifted up by strong arms. This time it was carried into a small church.

"Get ready," said T. Bear "I can't wait to stretch, and

shake out, and fluff up. I'm all smooshed and I want to look my best.

We're going to meet a lot of bears who have been sent here from all across America, just like us. We all want to be chosen to help the children."

The three friends were put on a table next to some stranger teddy bears. But, of course, stranger teddy bears don't stay strangers very long, do they? That's the best thing about a teddy bear. When you're with a bear you never feel alone.

"Hi, I'm Daisy" said one of the bears. "Me and my friends have come all the way from Michigan."

"Hi Daisy, I'm Cuddles. I'm from Iowa. I was sent here by a little girl named Sally. She's a people. Sally hugged every single bear in the whole store before she picked me off the shelf. She wanted the bear that she sent to be just right."

"Cuddles, how come you know all this stuff about what's happening with us anyway?" asked Daisy.

"My cousin Albert Bear told me," said Cuddles proudly. "He's already helping a little girl. Guess what was written on the note for his child?

Just in case you're feeling blue
I've got a great big hug for you

I liked that, and Albert did too. After we get our notes and are ready, we'll ride to a school where we'll meet the children.

It won't be much longer now, Daisy, before we meet the Bear Lady. Are you excited?"

"I sure am, Cuddles. I've never seen so many bears. All kinds of bears. All sizes. All colors. That bear's tag says he comes from New Mexico, from an Indian Reservation .

And look at the one with the fancy sunglasses! She must be from Florida or California! Will all of us be accepted, Cuddles?" I guess I'm worried because we're all so different."

"I hope so Daisy. But I'm mostly concerned about Gruff, and that tiny little blue bear. Do you think he's going to be big enough to give hugs to the children?"

"I don't know, Cuddles, I'm a little nervous myself. But I'm wondering more about how the children will feel. Will they be sad, or scared, or…or will they just need to talk, or to hug? You know, us teddy bears are the best listeners."

"Uh-oh, hush," warned T. Bear. "Here comes the Bear Lady. Now it's our turn! She's going to choose!

Look smart, Gruff, close your mouth. Don't say a word! Smile, Cuddles. Okay! Okay! She's holding me and it looks like I'm going to make it. She put me in the pile to get ready to go! Yep! I'm going. YEAH!"

T. Bear shouted to his friends from across the big pile of chosen teddy bears. "Bye, Cuddles, good luck. You know I believe in you! Good-bye, Gruff, you'll be fine. Just don't show your teeth."

Wait a minute, Gruff. Hold on. I think the Bear Lady is heading straight for you. She's smiling! Wow, Gruff, I think maybe she has something special in mind for you.

Is that a little red fireman's helmet? I think you're going to

a fire station. Maybe one of those stations that helped put out the fires on 9-11. You might even ride in the truck!"

Gruff's toothy grin and growl did not seem to be a problem anymore as he said proudly, "that's PERRFECT!"

Then T. Bear was carried outside and put in a car by a volunteer. For a long time he rode in the dark, not knowing where he was going.

Finally he could see they were driving into a city. Oh my, thought T. Bear, yes…it looks so scary…I see soldiers in the streets, and there's a tank in the middle of the city! No wonder my child needs me right by his side.

The car stopped and a big fireman lifted T. Bear up gently and handed him to a sad little boy.

Well. Hello there, You, thought T. Bear. Oh I like you so much! I know that I can be your friend. Would you like to be mine? Does he understand me? wondered T. Bear as he looked into the boy's eyes. He didn't have to wait long to find out.

My child grabbed me and hugged me so tight, marveled T. Bear. I could feel his little heart beating. Wow! I wish I could tell Cuddles· This is so great!

When T. Bear looked up, he saw that the big fireman had strapped that tiny blue bear to his helmet so he could have hugs, too!

This is the happiest day of my life, thought T. Bear, as the little boy carried him home.

I sure wish I knew where Cuddles could be. Perhaps she was sent to a Marine base, or someplace where the Army is shipping out.

On military bases Dads and Moms will come to their child's school all dressed in uniform, ready to leave for another country.

They say goodbye right there at school. The children know that it might be really dangerous and they're worried. Yes, they need us there for sure. That could be where Cuddles was sent.

The Bear Lady said there were many other places in the country where children needed

bears too. Not just here in New York City.

Maybe Cuddles went to an evacuation center out West, to help children recover from an earthquake, or a forest fire. Or she might be going to the Midwest after a bad flood, or a tornado.

Wherever she is, I know that she is doing her job. If you happen to see Cuddles, would you please let me know?

The End